HUMANITY'S RAGE

Or, How to Stop Blissful Ignorance and Start Worrying

SIERRA ERNESTO XAVIER

Grosvenor House Publishing Limited

All rights reserved
Copyright © Sierra Ernesto Xavier, 2023

The right of Sierra Ernesto Xavier to be identified as the author of this
work has been asserted in accordance with Section 78
of the Copyright, Designs and Patents Act 1988

The book cover is copyright to Sierra Ernesto Xavier

This book is published by
Grosvenor House Publishing Ltd
Link House

140 The Broadway, Tolworth, Surrey, KT6 7HT.
www.grosvenorhousepublishing.co.uk

This book is sold subject to the conditions that it shall not, by way of
trade or otherwise, be lent, resold, hired out or otherwise circulated
without the author's or publisher's prior consent in any form of binding or
cover other than that in which it is published and
without a similar condition including this condition being imposed
on the subsequent purchaser.

This book is a work of fiction. Any resemblance to
people or events, past or present, is purely coincidental.

A CIP record for this book
is available from the British Library

ISBN 978-1-80381-446-9

Contents

HUMANITY'S RAGE	1
PRELUDE TO THE RAGE	3
THE SHADE	9
THE SHADOW	41
POSTLUDE	57
HAVE THEY FORGOTTEN ME?	63
AUTHOR'S NOTE	71
APPENDIX: UNUSED NOTES FOR ENCOUNTER VII	79

HUMANITY'S RAGE

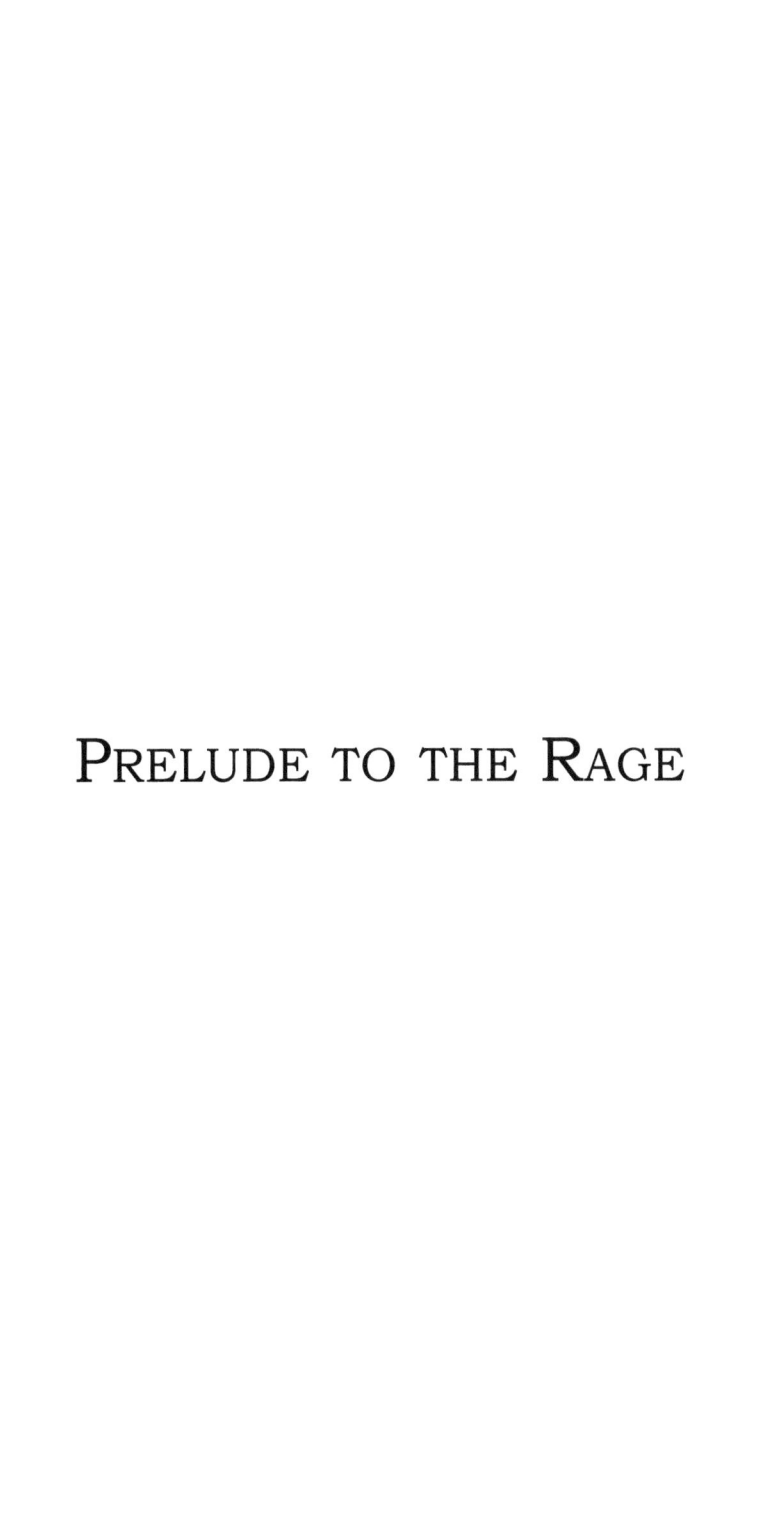

Prelude to the Rage

When we blink, we... we close our eyes, we close them to... to make the world obsolete, to... to hide away from it, to shut out the pain – yes, yes, we close our eyes to shut out the pain... And, and... and when we open them again, *and whilst they remain open*, we hear the voices of others, we hear the expressions of their humanity... their crying... their weeping... their sorrow... *It seems* that our eyes open to acknowledge these sounds of pain. Yet... yet we do not know precisely the direction from which the sounds come – just that we seem to hear them.

It is as if our eyes open instinctively as we hear these voices... instinctively so that we can try to establish where the calls from humanity are coming from. We hear the hurt in the voices of others as they express their anguish... and–and... and when we hear this anguish – we then close our eyes to it... we close them so that we can rest from all those voices, to hide away from all the pain, to hide away from what resonates within us – the pain we feel in empathy.

We have to rest because we are constantly being awakened to suffering, constantly being interrupted by the pleas from this humanity. But should we not rest in those momentary instances, those moments when our eyes are shut as we blink, then this pain might become too much for us.

For when our eyelids open and close each time we blink, they also lubricate our eyes... They, they make our vision clearer... they do this so that we can see, so that we can try and locate where the pain is coming from, and also to build up the tears in our eyes in empathy. With every cry we hear we accumulate more tears... tears to show that we are listening... tears to show that we are humane.

We have evolved, yes, *evolved*, to accumulate these tears, to be able to blink, so that we become aware when we hear humanity crying, so that we become aware when there is too much suffering out there, so that we can perhaps cry. We have also evolved to drain away these accumulated tears, to take them within ourselves, so that our bodies can carry the suffering.

But, when it is *our* voices that are suffering and when it is *our* tears that are shed... the nearness, the proximity, of this pain, of our own voices, causes *our* tears to build rapidly. Then... then for us, in the moment of our tears, to try harder... try harder to close our eyelids, so that we can shut out the hurt, so that we can shut out the hurt that is so close to our hearts.

That is why children cry... It is because they are not used to it... It is because their innocence lets them hear the cries of suffering from around the world. When they are born – they cry. They cry because it is the first time they have heard suffering... It is the first time they have heard the sound, the first time they have heard that uncomfortable sound... And, and... when this sound becomes too much for them – they fall asleep... They fall asleep because the crying and weeping of humanity overwhelms them... because their little minds and little bodies are overwhelmed... yes – overwhelmed... and then they take longer to recover – they take longer in their sleep so that they can recover.

We must hold these children. We must comfort them. We must do this. We must do this, whilst they hear the suffering, whilst they hear the pain. We must do this to let them know that there may be a future without these sounds.

But... but... but *it seems...* that as our children get old, as they get used to the cries, we let go of them... we no longer hold them, we no longer hold them as much... we let them know that this is the pain that they have to live with... this is the pain that they have to hear. We teach them that in the blink of their eyes, they will wake up to suffering and that there will be no one to comfort them, that there will be no one to help them understand the suffering, that they themselves will be alone. And by learning from us – as we let go of them, they themselves learn that they do not have to comfort others – comfort those who hear the suffering, comfort those who are suffering.

Our children will grow up to ignore the consolation of others, to ignore the sounds when their eyes are open – they will grow up to ignore the suffering... When – when they do grow up, when they are a little older... they will believe that looking away and ignoring the suffering is the norm. That holding them then will be a sign that *they* are in pain and not *others*.

As we grow up... our body adapts to keep these tears out of our eyes, to absorb the tears, to absorb the pain. We no longer want to weep, we choose not to weep at the suffering... but we allow our bodies to accept this suffering instead of consciously acknowledging it. And, and... and as we continue to get overwhelmed by it... we continue the need to sleep. We build up this pain, this hurt, this suffering that we carry with us... and we channel it into other means and forms – we get angry, we get annoyed, we hurt and irritate others... we choose to inflict the suffering we feel on others. Not only do we hear the suffering but we become perpetrators of suffering... we do this because, because we choose not to shed those tears... because... because we are weak. We are weak because we run away from what we should be listening to. We are weak because we choose to ignore that we are human.

We listen, we hear, we ignore and then we... we hurt.

THE SHADE

I

There was this fly, this... fly, this irritating fly ... it was...was bothering me... it bothered me... This fly – it was irritating me. It just flew and flew... around my head, around my eyes, invading my privacy – annoying me. It was minding its own business, doing what it was supposed to do... *to fly*.

But it wouldn't go away – it just wouldn't go... It kept bothering me... It kept hovering around my head, near my eyes and close to my ears... It just would not *go away*, and – and... and then... then it *landed... it landed* – this fly landed in front of me.

I looked at it, I looked at this fly... I looked at it.

Then, then... I then caught it, I – I caught it, I didn't kill it – I just caught it. I caught this – this little fly, this ... this fly that was bothering me... I caught it and... and I pulled its wings off – I didn't kill it – I just pulled its wings off – as if it was nothing... *nothing!*

It could no longer fly... It could no longer... bother me.

Imagine... Imagine if... if someone cut off your legs – pulled them clean off – as if they were nothing, as if they meant nothing... Imagine how you would feel... Imagine the pain, the suffering – the *suffering*... Imagine it – all those pain signals now rushing towards your brain. Imagine them... those pain signals rushing, *rushing*, *rushing* towards your brain, hitting your brain all at once, all at one time, at... at a single point in time. Can you imagine the intensity of that pain, of that suffering, of that emotional suffering?... Can you imagine it?

Imagine the psychological problems you would encounter... all those problems you would have to deal with – of having your legs pulled clean off... Imagine all the difficulties, the hurdles, all the suffering that you would have to face in that instant, in that single point in time. Now, imagine the psychological problems... that this fly has... the problems that I inflicted upon this fly.

The poor fly... the poor, poor *little* fly. I pulled its wings off – created an *immense* amount of *pain* and – and... and gave it *vast* amounts of psychological problems... so much *unwarranted* pain, so much *unwarranted* suffering, *because... because...* because it... *bothered* me...

I–I... I did it because *it bothered me*... I–I–I intentionally harmed it, *because... because it bothered me.*

II

I–I–I... I once saw a man... being hurt... He was being hurt in a way that makes you question... that makes you question our humanity... That you must question *why?*... *Why?*... Why?

I saw this man being hurt... hurt... hurt in a way that you would not want to be hurt. They... they... they were peeling his skin off... peeling it off his body... and then... then making him crawl... crawl with his skin hanging off. And – and it wasn't like the fly... it wasn't instantaneous... it was... it was... it was *slow*... *slow*... with the intent to torture.

I heard him scream, I heard him... O you should have heard him scream, how he screamed, he screamed. He screamed a painful scream – it was like no other... It was more painful than hearing a child cry in agony, crying in extreme pain... *screaming... in pain...* It was more desperate than – than a cry for help... It was a harrowing scream, *a scream*, almost... almost... insane.

I still hear it, I still hear it... Many moons later, I hear it.

Forgive me for crying, but you should have heard it – the scream of a man having his skin peeled off... and I saw this... I saw this with my own eyes and I cried – I cried, I cried, how I cried! I watched, I heard... and I cried.

You know, I can't understand it... I can't understand – I can't understand *why*... *why*... why people want to inflict... *inflict*... or *enjoy* hurting others... I just can't understand. But it was *that*... *it was just that*... *that* belief that there were people who liked doing such things... that people out there, for whatever reason, like doing such things... It took my breath away.

I watched this man being tortured. I heard his cries... *I watched someone INFLICT*... pain...on–on–on this man... and I just–just... just watched, *I just watched*... I *watched* a man suffer. I stood by and watched him suffer... I could have helped him, but I didn't... *I didn't help*... I just stood there... *crying*... watching him suffer... watching his pain.

Why? Why? ... *Why* did I not intervene? I was not chained, I was not restrained and I was free to do what I want, but *why*? Why did I stand back and watch? Why did my own humanity, when I could see suffering in front of my eyes, why... why did it allow me to watch and not intervene when I could have? *Why?* ... *Why?* ...

III

Some time ago, I do not know when, but some time ago... I saw some children – they were playing... playing games just like other children would do... they were just playing. You could hear the laughter; you could hear their giggles – they were just... just children.

When they were playing, they–they... they came across an animal, I cannot remember which animal – just an animal. They came across an animal and... and they looked at it, and as they looked at it, it moved... it *moved*. The animal moved and then they... *hit it*, they *hit it*. They *hit* the animal *with their sticks*, with pieces of broken wood – *they hit the animal with their weapons...* yes, *their weapons*. They killed this animal, they killed it and I heard its last cry... its cry of death.

And when this animal was dead, and you could see it was dead – when this animal was dead they continued to hit it – to beat it... they began to kick it... they kicked this dead animal... they kicked this dead animal that they had killed... they inflicted damage, yes damage – they continued to inflict this damage, they continued to inflict this humiliation and inflict it in an undignified, humiliating way... They killed an animal... and humiliated it.

I–I–I asked them why... why they did this... why had they killed this animal? ... And they, they... they replied – 'because they could'... *because they could*... because *they could*... Because they *felt they could*... they did what they did because *they felt*... they could. That their feelings gave them the justification for their action... that because of what they *felt*... it justified their action... it *justified* the killing of an animal, it justified the *murder* of an animal... that their feelings led them to an action... an action that would eliminate a life, that would damage a life.

Not at one moment, *and not at any moment*, did they... did they think *to question*... whether it was right to do so – whether it was *right*... to do so... They did not question their action. And by not *questioning* their action... by not *questioning*... they could *justify* what they *did* because... because... of a feeling.... By ignoring the need to question what they do – *their feelings*... *their feelings* justified the death of an animal, the death of a creature.

To this day, I do not understand *why*... I just do not understand *why*... *why* these children... *why* did they choose not to question... Why do people choose not to *question* what they *feel*?... I do not understand... I just do not understand.

IV

Many years ago, I remember... I remember... I remember being told, yes, I was told... told that... that all men were rapists – that – that all men were *potential* rapists.

I remember thinking – thinking how... how *amazing* it was. It was amazing: to say that all men, each and every man, was a rapist – *a potential rapist...* It was magnificent, yes, it was... *magnificent.* To reduce a whole gender... to define half of humanity – define it in terms of the use of their genitalia... Incredible! Absolutely incredible!

Do you see the magnificence of it? Do you?... That this splendour, this glorious idea, that this, this notion that... that the human race is defined by the use of their genitalia. That the... the magnificence of it is, is... that all men are *rapists...* and... and... and by the same defined logic... that... that... that all women are *whores... potential whores.*

Can you see it? Can you see the brilliance of it?... That we can reduce the whole of humanity – the whole of humanity, not just half of it – down to the functionality of their genitalia: one outwardly and aggressive and the other inwardly and openly all consuming... That this society, this world, this humanity is made up of... of *whores* and *rapists*... *RAPISTS AND WHORES*... That each and every one of us is... is... is a *RAPIST*... or a *WHORE*. That we *rape* and *whore* our way through life... raping others and whoring ourselves... raping and whoring, *WHORING AND RAPING*.

Look at your husband... your boyfriend... your son, your father... Look at your wife, your girlfriend... your daughter... and your mother... Then look at yourself in the mirror and see... see a potential whore or rapist. That's how screwed up this world is.

Fuck!... That's what we do, that's what we are... We are born FUCKERS!... We are all FUCKERS! Fucking rapists and fucking whores, fucking our way through life... And–and it then, then truly becomes a true case of evolution – survival of the fuckers!

Yes, yes, our biology... our biology tells us to rape, it tells us to *whore*, that... that we are... are *genetically... biologically engineered...* to *whore* and *rape*... That the moment we are born, we are born to rape and prostitute ourselves...

The sheer brilliance of that... the sheer brilliance...

V

This world... this, this world we live in... we... we abuse this world... we... we *abuse* this world we live in, we rape the land, we... rape it... we rape the land we think we own, and... and we build, *we build*... we build vast concrete jungles and support civilisations in them. We support these civilisations by... by... by polluting the seas, the air, the–the–the land... and we s-u-c-k out all the natural resources, we *suck* them right out... and we build monuments of–of–of grey ugliness, and machines of terror and torment... And... and YET, yet we SAY, *WE SAY, we say we see beauty*, that we see beauty, that we know what beauty is, that we know what it is. Do we? ... Do we know what beauty is?

We rule this world by our rage and anger – *with rage and anger*... towards our natural world... And we rule it in the name of *progress*... Yes, yes, we rape our world with rage and anger for... progress, *for progress*. Rage and anger for progress... And our *weapons* are WEAPONS OF TERROR... and TORMENT... We terrorise this world by our... '*progress*'... in the name of mankind, man-kind... Man... unkind...

We... we... we pride ourselves on success... on *suc*-cess... and–and... and with this success there is, there is, there is always a cost to another.... A cost, *A COST*... always a cost... That someone – some*one*... someone less fortunate... or weaker... *weaker*... weaker than ourselves... that someone weaker than ourselves will always pay the price of our success: that our governments – *our* governments – our governments want to dominate – *to dominate*... to dominate others economically, to be successful – to be successful economically... to... dominate... to gain extra *WEALTH*, to gain extra money... to gain this, to gain this – at the expense of others... to gain this whilst creating poverty elsewhere.

There is a certain rage... and anger... in the way we allow it to perpetuate, in the way we *want it* to perpetuate, for this gain, for this success and... and we justify it, we justify it as – as self-survival... and this – this... at the cost to others... To reign economic terror... over others... to bully... to bully others because... because of their lack of economic weight... because of their – their poverty... and we do it in the name of progress.

Then... then... when they... they disrupt our source, our source of growth, our source of success – our source of... dominance... We then... begin to dislike, *to dislike*... to... to... to *hate others*... for wanting to survive. That... that... that when it affects us we get... *concerned*... we get concerned that someone is depriving us of our dominance... then... then our fellow *humans* – yes, our *fellow humans* – then... then our fellow humans become the preventers of our freedom: they are no longer victims of poverty but... but a threat to our freedom, a threat to our dominance, a threat to our success.

Because, because we need to maintain – maintain our success... we... we... we do not give *sufficient* aid to these... these countries where poverty exists... we do not give sufficient aid until – until they... they open up their borders, their markets... We do not give aid, sufficient aid – unconditionally... We do not give it out of the goodness of our hearts, we give – we give... we give it so that we can have something from others... we give it because it serves *our* purpose, because it *serves us*... We do not give because it is right to do so, we don't do that... we... we don't do that... we... we have to maintain some form of advantage. We bully and barter so that we can get an edge, a... a competitive advantage over the poor, over those less fortunate than us... We make aid, we – we make it, we make it conditional for this – this aid... We *bully – we bully*... This bullying, this terror, this torment – of the poor – is part of our success, part of our dominance.

That is our human nature; that is the way we are – mankind: bigger, better, better than the rest – ruling this world with anger, rage and terror... and use this anger, this... rage... and this terror to perpetuate poverty... to perpetuate suffering... We rule it, we rule this world with this rage, with this torment, with this terror, this anger, we rule it and *yet*, and *YET*, we say, we *SAY, we say we believe in human rights.*

Because we *allow* it to happen, because we *want* it to continue, because we want the advantages, we also want the suffering and poverty to continue. We must *therefore* enjoy the methods by which we maintain this advantage, this success – this anger, rage and *terror*. We must therefore *approve of them*, approve the *use* of them and when we do, when we do, then we must ask how we can believe in human rights. If we enjoy this anger, rage and terror... how do we *define* what is *right*?... How do we *define* what is human?

That's where it lies, that's where it lies... How... how can we be 'civilised', how can we be *civilised*, how can we be *human*... knowing... *knowing... knowing* that the rudeness of poverty... the... the... the *rudeness* of suffering exists in this world... and... and... and we can allow it to continue so long as we have the extra *buck*, the extra *dollar* in our *pockets*... That... that my dollar is worth someone else's suffering, that it is worth someone else's poverty... It is *OBSCENE*, it is... *OBSCENE.*

Yet, yet, with this icon of success – with this icon, this – money... with this dollar, this dollar I can... I can... I can even pay someone; pay someone this sign of success and pay them to kill someone else, to rape someone – to have sex with someone, to murder... yes, to murder and they will do it, they *will* do it... they will do it because, because it is their... their criteria of success... success at the expense of others.

How... how can we rule this world... on... on an individual basis... on a governmental basis... on an economic basis, on any *basis* and ALLOW such *OBSCENITIES* to continue? *How can we do this? How can we do this? How can we do this* and be so far from being human?

It is *primeval...* It is our primordial instinct – *to fight... to fight* and *succeed* at the expense of others... to trample over those who are *weaker* and less fortunate... than ourselves... It is our animal instinct and, yes... we are animals, more so than human – we, we, we do not exercise our ability to distinguish right from wrong – we know it exists but we choose not to change the systems by which we live. We... We are complicit in all this... because... we choose not to change these systems.

We are truly... more animal than we think we are... We... we are therefore *not... not* as evolved as we think we are... and it is only our *arrogance... OUR ARROGANCE...* that makes us feel superior... to the rest of the animal kingdom.

It is our arrogance – *our arrogance*, that ... that causes these obscenities.

Can there be beauty in this?

VI

Justice! ... Justice! ... There is no justice – there are only opinions... opinions and *judgements*... opinions and judgements... *of people*... people who believe they know what justice is.

Justice?... Is there any justice?... Is there any justice for being a great man?... For being a man of war, a great man of war, to sanction the deaths of many... for a war... *Why do we arrest those who protest for peace*... and not those men who seek war? How can you be great? How can you be great... for sending men to war?

Alexander is considered great... but to the Persians... to them... to them he is a man who *raped*, *murdered* and *tortured* their families, their children. But you will say he did it for some noble reason – yes, yes, he *nobly* raped, he *nobly* murdered and he *nobly* tortured men, women and children. Alexander is truly a great man... he is a great man of *rape*, *murder* and *torture*.

And how come it is our young *MEN* we send to war... how come we send them to war *so easily*?... That we say that their *balls* are not worth saving, and yet, *and yet*, if we had an army of women – their *tits* would be seen as invaluable and war less attractive.

Justice!... Where is justice?... Where is justice when eight hundred thousand people die, when *eight hundred thousand* people are murdered in one hundred days, in just *one hundred days*? Where is the justice of these eight hundred thousand people?... Eight thousand people murdered per day, *eight thousand* – the equivalent of fourteen and a half million people being murdered during a five-year world war – *fourteen and a half million.* Where is the justice in that? When *eight thousand die a day* and the world sleeps! Where is the justice when people *do not even know* that eight hundred thousand deaths occurred in one hundred days, that people do not even know what the deaths refer to, but are aware of what cosmetic surgery a celebrity has had? Those eight hundred thousand Rwandan deaths mean nothing compared to a pair of celebrity tits! Where is the justice in that?

Where is the justice when six *million, SIX MILLION... Jews* die... and... and *TWENTY MILLION, TWENTY... MILLION ... Russians...* twenty million Russian deaths go unnoticed, unacknowledged, and are not given... equal *v-a-l-u-e*, equal *r-e-s-p-e-c-t...* in the annals of *history...* It is as if their *sacrifice...* is *unreal...* or *untrue...* Where... where is the justice in that?

Where is the justice in making us feel sad... making us feel guilty... to feel remorse... to *feel* horrified about the six... to feel horrified about the six, when *in fact* we should feel *horror* and *disgrace* about the twenty-six, where is the justice in that? Where is the justice? That because of their ethnicity, their religion, their nationality, their political persuasion, we do not give equal *respect* – to their deaths.

That *IF* one man dies... compared to six or twenty dying, then that is of an equal disgrace... That we must acknowledge that it is neither the quantity nor the means by which deaths occur, but the respect of a death – the extinguishing of a life – whether it be one, two or many. That if we choose to ignore... if we choose not to...to give equal weight, to give equal value, to some who have died – then we do not do justice... to our fellow beings... to humanity.

Because, *because*... we do not value life, we do not value life equally... we... we do not know what... what *justice* really is.

VII

I was blind once, I did not question it – I allowed myself to be blind... and when I began to see – I closed my eyes.

Truth... There is no truth – there are only victims. Victims of twisted logic. There are lies... lies... lies everywhere.

I saw a film once... I saw a film about death – death and destruction... I saw it... *I saw it* with my own eyes... I saw this film, this government/military film... I saw the film of people dying... I saw deaths... *I witnessed the shame, I witnessed* this stain on humanity – I witnessed it with my own eyes.

My eyes saw, they saw *death... death... death* on a grand scale, *en masse*, death en masse... thousands – hundreds of thousands of deaths... hundreds and thousands of deaths in... in just a few seconds... hundreds of thousands wiped out – DEAD... in a few seconds.

Yet, *yet*... they did not record this film to show the deaths of many... They recorded it to show the *efficiency*... of a weapon of terror... The use of this weapon had to be recorded... and not the deaths of much of humanity.

It perpetuated A LIE... a lie so subtle... a lie so great – *great* in its ambitions... *great* in its scope... I saw this lie unfold in front of my eyes... and it is *ENOUGH... ENOUGH to question...* to question whether there is truth... whether truth can really exist.

The lie, this lie, there are so many lies... I saw it, I saw a weapon of defence – a *weapon* to protect our country – they did not say it was a weapon of terror, they said it was a weapon of *defence...* that somehow the death and destruction of thousands, hundreds of thousands of people *is* a weapon of defence... *It is a weapon...* a weapon – it kills, it destroys... *and yet* I am to believe it is a friendly weapon... a friendly weapon that destroys humanity in a few seconds.

That it is *a* weapon – it is *one* weapon – a singular entity, just one – it is a single weapon... But I saw, I saw, and what they do not tell you is... that this *ONE* is equivalent to hundreds of thousands of deaths... that somehow they forget to tell you about the hundreds of thousands, and they just want you to focus on the one... *and it is this...* this insult to humanity... that they wish to perpetuate. That they can show a weapon from a *distance,* something that is remote, something that does not need to affect us... but they will *not* show the moments of deaths, of all these deaths, of our fellow humans... of people like you and I who die within a few seconds – they will not show you that... That somehow ONE is the truth and that the hundreds of thousands are forgettable, just like pieces of shit being flushed down a toilet – irrelevant.

What is *obscene*... is that these weapons, these weapons of terror and torment, continue... continue to be built... Built and designed to be more clinical... to be more efficient... to kill more and more people with *greater* ferocity in a shorter and shorter space of time... in even fewer seconds... That this, THAT THIS and the *need* for more efficient and more clinical weapons are – are noble justifications to build these weapons of terror, to build them for the sake of humanity... to build these machines of terror that kill millions... millions... rather than hundreds of thousands... for the sake of humanity.

That it is companies that design and build these weapons... and that these companies, these companies *compete* with one another... that they *compete* to get government *contracts*... Companies that compete in creating newer and better, more efficient methods of death... that these companies compete for the efficiency of death... and we celebrate this by awarding them contracts... And... and... and how is the building of more efficient methods of death by these companies... how is this any different from the efficient methods of death in the Holocaust, apart from being more efficient and more clinical? That... that the 'final solution' to humanity can be privatised... to make profit in death.

Do you not see... do you not see?... That the film was never about the truth... It is about a lie... about a lie.

That we can see... and view... a *film* of a clinical method of destruction... that we can detach ourselves clinically from the many deaths that occur... And because we can detach ourselves, we can turn away from the consequences... we can stop the film, we can put our mugs of coffee down on the papers whose headlines we want to remain detached from... that we can switch off our news channels because our lunch, our dinner, our evening *meals* are more important to us than the deaths of thousands... that by not seeing, by not viewing, we can erase it from our minds – that we can erase it from history... that we can erase humanity.

It is this, this self-deception, this lie – that we would prefer not to know the truth than to confront it. That we lie to ourselves is what makes me want to scream... *scream* because... because it is so – so... so dangerous. But, we do that, we do that – we deceive ourselves, we hide ourselves from the truth because... because... our lunches are too important.

VIII

I don't know. I... don't *know*... I *don't* know... I just... don't know.

IX

I... I... I woke up... yes, I remember... I remember now... I – I... I woke up with blood, yes blood... blood on my hands... It's – it's all too vague, but I knew, *I knew... I knew...* I knew I had to... I just... had to... They would not, they... just would not... would not agree, agree with – with me... They just – would not.

Yes, yes... yes I know it is wrong... it is wrong to... to *bludgeon*, yes – bludgeon... people to death... I–I know it is wrong to – to... to kill... yes, kill... kill because, because people *do not* agree with you – I know it is wrong.

You know, you know... I did this once before... I... I... I got angry, *very angry...* got angry because... because they – they *laughed... because they laughed.* They, they laughed... they, they... would not stop... they *would not* stop. They just – just kept laughing... they kept laughing. They kept laughing at me... *laughing at me... BUT* they could not – they could not – or rather, they... they would not... *understand...* they would not understand *that – that I* was different... different from them.

But I... I... I could, I could understand this... I... I... I could understand them... I... I could accept this and I could *e-v-e-n* accept them... I could even, even... even accept their laughter, their laughter... But *what* I could not accept was the *fact... the fact...* the fact that they called me... they called me a 'coward'... *a coward*, a... coward.

They should not have done this; they really should not have done this... I could not help it... I–I could not help it... I just – just... just could not... I–I–I... went *mad...mad...* yes, mad... mad with *anger... anger and rage.* Yes, yes... with anger and rage... But... but they still – laughed... they, they laughed... they would not stop – *they laughed.* They just would not stop... They laughed... *they laughed at me – AT ME... They laughed at ME...* at... at calling me a coward... A... *coward...* They laughed at me because... because to them... *to them...* I was... was a coward.

But this was, was... was too much, too much... *for me...* it was just too much...I–I... I even told them that... that I was *not, I was not...* I was not a coward... *But, but...* but they did not agree... They – they... just did not agree... They did not agree with me – and... and I–I... I had to stop them... to stop them from calling me a coward, *from calling me...* a coward.

So I–I ... I *picked up...* picked up a girl, a little girl... a... a... a little baby girl – and broke her neck... I broke her neck and then... then... when she was dead – I battered her... I battered, yes, battered her and broke every single bone in her body... I broke every single bone in her little body... *when she was dead.*

You see, you see, I... I... I killed a baby... a little, little baby... not only because they would not agree... but because... because... because of laughter, *laughter, their laughter*... because they were laughing... laughing *at me*... and because their laughter had *bothered me – it bothered me*... it bothered me and... and... and also because... because of the word... the word 'coward'.

I killed because...because of a word, because of this word – 'coward'... I killed because of a word... I KILLED, I MURDERED for a word – *I took* away a human life... a *human life*... I committed an act of violence – of savagery... for a word... Just – just a word... a word just like any other – but with a different meaning, but *nevertheless* – a word... This, this word... the word 'coward'... I KILLED for a word... That is what I did... KILLED... MURDERED... for a word... for a... a... word... a word that *bothered* me.

But do not judge me by it... do not judge me. You may not have liked what I have said, but do not judge me... It may have bothered you – but do not judge me... You do not have to listen to me... you do not have to *listen*... You can turn your head away – you can close your eyes to me, you can do that... You can go hide... *hide*... in the shade... hide... hide... hide and attend to your lunches.

I... I... I once... I once fucked a girl, a little girl – she was twenty, but she looked like a little girl. I once fucked this girl – this beautiful girl... I fucked her... I fucked her hard... I fucked, we fucked – we fucked hard... Fucked and fucked... we fucked so hard; we fucked until I bled, we fucked until she bled, we fucked until we both bled... *Fucked* and *fucked* until we both bled – that fucking whore *paid me* to fuck her, to fuck her like a rapist... Then... then... then I... I... I killed her... I killed her... killed her with my... my hands – the same hands that gave her pleasure – I killed her with my *hands*... I–I–I suffocated her... I–I suffocated her because... because... because I–I loved her – I loved my little whore... Yes, yes – I loved her... I... I... I loved her.

She... she... she told me she had... had... had cancer – that she had cancer... I... I... I killed her... I killed her because... because... I... I... I did not want her to suffer – to... to suffer... I had to kill her, I had to... I killed her because... because I loved her... I killed because... I was in love – I did it without questioning, without thinking... I did it because I... *felt*... because I *felt* love for her... *I killed* out of love, *because of the way I felt*, and she even *paid me* to do it, *she paid me to do it... she paid me.* Don't you just love capitalism? To earn money in killing.

You see, I fucked – I fucked a... a little girl... this, this beautiful girl... *I fucked her...* I FUCKED this – this girl, I FUCKED her... FUCK, that's what

I did – FUCK... FUCK, FUCK, FUCK what a FUCKING stupid word 'FUCK' is... FUCK – that's what I did – FUCK... I FUCKED for love... I FUCKED this girl because, because I *loved* her.

Then it occurred to me – it *occurred to me*... Imagine... *Imagine*... Imagine what I would have done if I had hated her.

I knew, I knew... I knew I had to punish... yes, to punish... punish myself... Yes, yes, I had to... to... to suffer, suffer as she did... suffer... suffer for my sins. I do not want to rot, to die in a cell – to be incarcerated – I do not want that... Therefore, *therefore*... I must... *must*... punish myself.

When... when... when I do want to punish myself, to seek justice upon myself, just as if any other criminal would be punished, it is I who is seen as... as mad... I am not mad – I just want to be punished... punished for my sins.

I got in touch with people... these, these people... these people who wanted me to suffer... They wanted me to – suffer.

I... I punished myself by... by buying torture... Torture... Torture that our governments will be proud of... Torture that will be inflicted by kids... little kids – SCUM. If they were paid for it, these kids – these scum, these wonderful little kids... these kids would even... would even *fuck* their own mothers, would *rape* them, would fuck them as if they were whores – they would *kill* their fathers, their *own* fathers... and for what?... for money... They would FUCK and KILL, KILL and FUCK, FUCK for money, KILL for money, FUCK and KILL for money, for this – this money... and what is this money?... This money is... is... is paper... They would FUCK and KILL, KILL and FUCK, FUCK for paper, KILL for paper, FUCK and KILL for paper, for this – this paper... for... for... for paper.

Yet, yet... I gave them this... this paper... this money... I gave them this paper... to make me suffer... I *bartered*... I *bartered* paper for suffering... Paper... Paper... Suffering.

So who were these... these boys and girls, these little kids? ... Little kids – no hopers; the down-and-outs... society had failed to provide for them... yes... yes, it failed. Poor little shits, that's what they were – little... *shits*... shits that people would walk all over... But they rebelled – rebelled for their sakes – rebelled and became mercenaries... kids... just kids, little kids... kids who became *mercenaries*... kids... kids... kids who wanted to do what these fat cats in their offices were doing, though not in commerce, but in torture... they wanted paper.

I paid these little shits, these kids, these mercenaries. *I paid them*... paid them to... to make me suffer... and they did... they made me suffer.

These kids... these kids stripped me – they took away my clothes... they... they wrapped me in ... in barbed wire – in barbed wire... they wrapped me in this... and they made me suffer: they *punished me*... They, they pushed me... pushed me... pushed me on my sides... and rolled me... Rolled me up and down a hill, up and down... up... and down... They did this... did this for hours... hour after hour... after hour, tearing and ripping my skin – my flesh, my flesh.

They ripped out... ripped out my nails from their sockets – on my feet, on my hands... Then... then... then they whipped me... they whipped me, they whipped me a hundred times – *a hundred times*... and then, then, they put salt all over me... The tears flowed from my eyes.

They poured water over me... they poured water and... attached electrical wires... They gave me shocks – electric shocks... one after another, shock after shock, pain after pain – and they... they continued until I nearly died.

These shits, these bastards, these little bastards... little kids – that's who they were – little kids... little kids *who were so young* that they did not even know the meaning of the word MASTURBATION... These little shits – these shits were torturing me... making me *suffer*... *suffer* as I asked... and all for what?... For... *paper*... for *paper*.

How wonderful this paper is!... Enough for you to think that I... I *deserved* such suffering – to deserve suffering *because*... because I *killed... I killed and battered* a baby girl... *to deserve suffering* because... because I *fucked* and *killed* a woman... But what is this... this 'deserve', apart from being a word?... What is it?...'Deserve'... 'Deserve'... deserve is like... like you saying... saying you want to watch suffering... that you want to watch *me* suffer... to... to... to ignore *humanity*... to... to... to ignore it and to be inhumane, to be inhumane by watching suffering, by watching *me* suffer.

Do I 'deserve' this? Do I?... Do I deserve it for battering a baby girl? To batter a creature, an animal, after I had killed it?... Do I *'deserve'* it... for killing a young woman – for having *fucked her* until we both bled?... Would you...would you... would you intervene as you watched me suffer? Would you listen to your humanity?

You do not even know if what I have said is the truth. You do not even know if you have been sold a lie, whether you have been sold the 'one' or the many.

But did you *even – even... at any time...* seek to question what you have heard?

The Shadow

X

We must *weep*, we must... *weep*... For if we do not... then our children, *our children* – they will only know what darkness is. They will... only see darkness. They will... be used to this darkness... and for them, *for them*... opening their eyes, their *eyes* – they will believe that darkness is what you see when you open your eyes.

They will not see the truth. They will not question. They will not seek justice. They will walk in darkness... We must *therefore*... weep... we must weep... to... to show them that we know what compassion is...

Our tears, *our tears*... our tears will show them... they will show them that even though... even though there is darkness all around... that we... *we*... we know what compassion is. That *we know* and *they must* not forget... That the lies may persist... but so will our tears.

XI

It seems strange... that our... our *beliefs* are what destroy us. That our own... *beliefs*, our own *ideas*, our own *thoughts*... It is they that defeat us.

That these thoughts, these... ideas, these beliefs... are natural – they are natural. That they are natural phenomena, yes – they are natural: something that we just do – like a blink of an eye. That this naturalness... *is*... is a part of our make-up... something that is a given, a given for who we are... a given for being human, that by being human we must, by our very nature, think.

It is these thoughts, these ideas, these beliefs – it is these that destroy us... It is our humanity that destroys us... It is what makes us human that destroys us... We... we die – we die because of ourselves, because by being who we are we have thoughts that destroy us.

That, that... people throughout history have gone to war... and have died for their cause... that they have died for their beliefs, that their beliefs have destroyed them. Yet, *yet*... I–I have to give up my cause, my beliefs... just to prevent my own destruction.

These thoughts, these ideas... I am not talking about the ideas and beliefs, my views of destruction and violence; I am not just talking about them – but my striving towards these thoughts and my need to attain what I think. Some... some would say that it is a want, a desire that I create to attain my thoughts... and... and... and that as I have these thoughts I must... must invariably want or desire them.

These thoughts, these ideas, my thoughts, my ideas – they destroy me... they... de-stroy me... That... what I believe: that I should not harm others because I am human; that I should not stand by and do nothing when I see suffering, when I see obscenities; that I should be striving for justice and a just world. That I should do all these because... because it is right to do so... that as I have a conscience... as I have the ability to exercise – 'morality'... that I do so... that I do so because a failure to do so... a failure... would mean a failure of myself as human.

It is this... it is... this, this belief that we must strive to exercise what it is in us... what it is in us that is human... It is this, this... this idea that causes me so much... pain, so much agony... to want to see ourselves act... act and be our distinctive human selves. It is that, that prevents me from being non-unhappy. That... it is not because I cannot obtain it, but because... because I choose not to.

When... when I–I–I try, I am swimming against the tide... swimming against an... ocean current – that it exhausts me, that it tires me... it tires me mentally, it tires me as I face those who choose not to exercise our humanity. By... by wanting what I do, by wanting humanity... I am... unhappy... That the desire... that I have... the desire that I generate – to attain this... causes my misery. It is enough... enough to make you feel, to make you feel... cold and lonely... enough to question, question your existence... enough to make you want to weep – to make you want to cry.

It is strange... it is strange that by wanting such a thing, such an idea... that I am defeated by my own belief. That it is my thoughts... that defeat me... That my desire... *my desire*... for a better humanity... defeats me.

That if I no longer struggle or strive for this – I no longer get disappointed... I no longer endure... *endure*... the *frustration*... I no longer lose faith, yes, faith in humanity because... because my expectations are of an unjust world... a world where we are... reluctant to take action... when we see wrong... and a world of greed and terror, where we can harm others and have no compassion... no compassion... towards people who are different from ourselves.

When I accept this... when I accept this... I am less unhappy... I am... less unhappy... That pragmatism... *pragmatism*... pragmatism seems to triumph... triumph over idealism. And yet, yet I know... I know deep down, *deep down*... that,

that... pragmatism will never improve this world... would never improve humanity. That when I *fuck*... I do not fuck for the benefit of mankind, I do not *fuck* for the benefit of my partner... I fuck for myself.

XII

My tears – they have dried… I cry… I cry inside… but my tears… my tears – they are dry.

There… there… there is a loneliness that I feel, a coldness that runs through my body.

What am I?… Who am I?… I–I… I am… I am no longer in need of a better humanity… and… and… and I feel like a piece of human excrement – a waste… a total waste… that a need for a better humanity… is… is… wasted – gone. Gone… What's left?… What is left?… just human sewage…

XIII

Do you know?... Do you *know*... what it feels like to be lost?... To be lost within yourself... It–it–it is... is like a feather, a *feather*... in amongst... a turbulent... wind... Yes, a feather, a feather... in amongst wind... No control... no control over your destiny... no respect for who you are... Beaten... beaten by what is around you... Fear! ... Fear!... fear – because you have no control – no shape or direction to your life... Sadness... sadness at your *own* helplessness... *Because... because* you are just a... a feather.

XIV

Can you imagine... history, beginning of time... all that pain... all that suffering... the endless empires... the endless wars... the hatred? Can you imagine it?

Imagine – people dying... the number of people dying... the pain and the hurt and the suffering in the moments of their deaths... Can you hear their screams? Can you hear their pain? Can you hear the pain of humanity? Can you?

Imagine... imagine... the bullets... the machetes... the sounds of all those arrows, of all those spears... all the hacking... every stabbing... and the torture, *yes*, the torture.

Those children... all those children dead... all those people dead... *DEAD*! They all died because... because... of their religions, their beliefs, their gender, their... their differences – yes, their... differences.

And does knowing this... make you want to weep, or does it make you want to... look away?

Can you imagine... the glimpses of life – the moments of death... all those points of pain, all those moments of suffering? Can you imagine them... all of them... from the beginning... year after year, millions upon millions... being *felt*, being *heard*... being *experienced* all at once?

Are we... human? Are we truly... human?

XV

Our lives are like cobwebs... we just cling from one wall to another... waiting... waiting for a creature to come – waiting for happiness, waiting for a creature... a creature... caught, entangled... upon our web... making an impression on our lives.

Then... then... by *some chance*, by some chance we... we lose grip on one of our walls... and are left dangling... desperate... desperately holding on... And... and... all it takes is... is a strong wind, a few raindrops... to dislodge us... to make us lose our grip on that remaining wall.

We lose our grip like we lose our lives... we disappear into nowhere – nobody knows, nobody cares... We're just another life, another cobweb... that has disappeared... disappeared from time... without a trace... superfluous to the walls... irrelevant to history.

XVI

I–I–I once looked at this nail, this three-inch nail – I once looked at it close up... It was... it was on a table, upright... nothing... nothing else around it... nothing else on that table – nothing... This nail, this three-inch nail – it looked lonely, *it looked* – lonely... lonely... cold and lonely... just as I had felt.

I had felt lonely... a loneliness that you cannot understand, that you cannot know how to understand... You cannot understand because... because it is not simply about being around others... it is not about the proximity of others... It is about your heart... your heart being detached from you.

Perhaps love would help?... But how much love can you give a nail?... How much love can you give me?... Can a nail receive love? Can I?

I–I feel too lonely... too lonely to accept love... It is like dying of thirst – dying of thirst in a desert: where you cannot drink water immediately... you cannot drink it immediately, because – because, it will be a *shock*, a *shock to your system*... That is loneliness... when... when... when accepting love... is a shock to your system.

How do you escape from that? How do you?

This nail... This nail, standing upright on this empty table... *looked*... looked *so lonely*, so lonely when I looked at it close up. This nail, this nail looked so big, so painful, so powerful and so lonely... And... and... and when I saw how big, how painful it was I–I... I raised my hand and with *all the force and strength I had* I–I–I slammed my hand right down on top of the nail, I slammed it, I slammed it with brute force and yes I had pain, I had pain, how I had pain, but that pain, the pain, it let me know, it let me know that I existed, that I existed in amongst that loneliness, I *existed*... so that I did not have to become like that nail – so cold, so lonely. *Even... even* though it was a momentary existence, a momentary pain... at least... at least I could... acknowledge it... acknowledge my... existence.

XVII

You know... There comes... There comes a time in a man's life where... where... where things get... get... just too much – too much for a man to cope... where – where his – his cries go unheard, where his cries of pain go unheard.

There comes a time in a man's life... where... where... where the suffering gets too much, where–where... where life itself is too much to handle... where you can't endure much more pain... This is the point, *this-is-the-point*, the point where no one can really blame you... That is the point... That is the point that I have reached.

You see... A man can only suffer so much – he can only endure so much suffering, so much pain, so much hardship. And once past this point... he–he reaches desperation... and if he is alive he wants to die... die because... because his cries of help go unheard, unanswered... can you blame me for wanting to die? Paralysed by the fact that no one can help. Left alone to rot, to suffer – his mind darkened.

XVIII

I have glimpsed death, I have seen it... I have been there – the edge of life, suicide.

Death... Death... Death is like... like a shadow over your eyes...

Postlude

When we sleep we... we... we close our eyes, we close them so that we no longer have to hear the sound of pain, so that we no longer have to see the darkness.

We sleep... we sleep even when we are awake: we hide ourselves in the shade by averting our eyes from the brightness; we hide ourselves by turning our heads away in order to accept things as they are, just so that we can get on with our lives. It is in those moments, when we look the other way, when we do not question where the pain comes from, that it becomes easier for us to sleep than to face a mountain.

And in this 'awaking' sleep, we... we accept the darkness... we, we... we accept this darkness around us, we accept it for our children. And because we do this, because we accept this, our children will not know the true degree of brightness that can exist. They will only know a dimmer reality... a dimmer reality *because*... because we have chosen it as expediency to get on with our lives. An expediency that will allow us to forever hand down to generations phrases that we use... phrases like 'it is not like it used to be'... phrases like 'life was better when we were younger'. And it is phrases such as these that will be passed on through expediency just because... because we can not be bothered.

In this dimness, our children will not experience the freedoms we once knew, they will not know the brightness that we experienced. We will look at them, we will look at them and tell them... we will tell them that *'times have changed'* and that we cannot get back to the brightness that we as youngsters had known. And... and by doing this... our world will get darker as we begin to sleep longer.

Our children... our children... they will see this level of dimness; *they will see it...* as their brightness. That this darkness is their heritage, that it is our legacy... a gift to them. And, and... and they themselves will turn their heads, as we have taught them, only to look at a further dimness.

Because we care so little for our children's future, for our babies' future, we... we no longer sleep to recover from the pain we hear, we no longer sleep to recuperate from our daily physical endeavours, nor to reorganise in our minds what we have processed or thought during the day, we sleep to avoid the level of dimness that exists around us. We sleep to avoid knowing that we are so lovingly giving this darkness to our children's future. We... we... we are clearly blinded by the darkness we are content with.

But it is then, it is *then*... during our sleep... that we begin to dream, to dream about our future, about our hopes and about our aspirations. And unless we stand up and take action, unless we stop sitting in silence and unless we stop looking the other way, our dreams become meaningless, meaningless in that moment when we open our eyes and see the dimness that we have accepted. Our dreams will become meaningless not just for ourselves, but for our children, and for our children's children, because they will follow our example in accepting a darker shade of reality.

We must dream and we must act upon our dreams. We must do this so that we can let them know that there is a brighter world. We must do this so that we can let them know that there is a brighter future: a world in which we can hold our children; a world in which they will know what compassion is; a world in which they will know the meaning of love. And it is our duty to allow them to breathe safely, to encourage their smiles and to enable them to know the true extent of the level of brightness that can exist. We must dream to prevent a shadow from being cast over their lives.

There's a time when the operation of the machine becomes so odious, makes you so sick at heart that you can't take part! You can't even passively take part! And you've got to put your bodies upon the gears and upon the wheels, upon the levers, upon all the apparatus - and you've got to make it stop! And you've got to indicate to the people who run it, to the people who own it - that unless you're free the machine will be prevented from working at all!

Mario Savio
Sproul Hall
The University of California at Berkeley
2 December 1964

Have They Forgotten Me?

Have they forgotten me? Have they forgotten me? Do they not remember me? Can they not see me? Can they not hear me? Do they not care for me? Have they forgotten me? Have they forgotten me?

There is a dead man in this room. He is the only man in this room. He is a lonely dead man. This dead man has died kneeling down. He has died with his face in his hands. Why does the dead man remain in that position? Nobody knows. Nobody seems to care. Who is he? Who is this dead man? Has he been forgotten?

This man is *Hu*-man. He is a dead *Hu*-man. He is a dead human. He is a dead human being.

He is our forefathers. He is our ancestral heritage. He is our humanity: evolved; developed; destroyed. He is me. I am this *Hu*-man. I am this man, this dead man.

You kept me in the room. You did not care for me. You let me sit there and weep. You closed the door on me. You let me know that my voice was not to be heard, and if it was, it would only be when you opened the door: when you could tell others you were listening to me; when you could tell others that these tears, that these problems, are the cause of my pain; that you could therefore stop my pain by preventing me from weeping. You would seek your funding this way.

My voice became a murmur in the background whilst you sought some concrete evidence of me as a physical being, but you did not see me as a human being. You may have mapped out my genes but you had forgotten me. You did not hear me.

The only time you open the door is to show people that I am crying. So that you can say to them, 'We have to find out why he is crying'. When you have found out why, you will say, 'we need to find a solution to prevent these tears'. Once you have prevented them I can no longer cry. I become like you – incapable of crying. You can then applaud and set me free from that room. But there is a dead man left in that room. He is a dead man. I am the dead man.

You say you have progressed in the name of science. You may have found a solution to something that you thought you should fix. You may have found the answer to my ills and sufferings. You may have done that but you have destroyed me.

I am imperfect. You are perfect. I am an imperfect man. You are a perfect man. I am an imperfect human being. You are a perfect human being. You are a perfect being – a being that is perfect. A perfect being who no longer suffers, who no longer knows of suffering.

You are a perfect being who has been engineered to be intelligent, to think in straight lines. You will be engineered not to get ill, not to have any forms of mental illness. Your thoughts will always be linear: no more curves, no more circles. You will be incapable of being depressed. You are a perfect intelligent being who knows not of sadness. A being who does not need to grieve, who cannot grieve. You are a perfect intelligent being who does not know what unhappiness is. You cannot cry – you cannot shed a tear. You are perfect in the way that you do not know what these things are. You are perfect because you cannot feel them. And because you cannot feel them you cannot understand these feelings in others. You cannot understand the imperfect being. You cannot understand other people's sadness. You can neither understand their poverty nor their suffering. You – a perfect being – cannot understand compassion. You may try to observe it but you cannot understand it.

Your compassion is to try and make *me* less imperfect, to push ahead by unnatural means, to push ahead by unnatural selection. To force a pace of change without knowing the consequences, except that I will not shed another tear.

You will give me white teeth. My hair will no longer be grey. I shall forever be slim. I may be ninety-five but I will always look thirty. I will be free from disease but you will still feed me your *Franken*-food.

You are so perfect that you will pursue with all your resources any tears that I may show; whilst my brothers, on the other side of the world, will desperately search to pick up a few grains and seeds in dry crumbling soil, under a burning sun, so that their families can eat.

You want to be perfect. You are perfect. You continue with your paralysed thinking and soon will want my brothers to be perfect, perfect according to your perfection. Perfect just like you. Soon, they will lose their language. Soon, they will lose their culture. Soon, they will forget their heritage. Everyone will be perfect. Everyone will be forgotten.

> We will be the dead people,
> We will be the forgotten people,
> No more than an ancient memory,
> Lost in amongst the rain,
> Lost in amongst the fog.

You are not a perfect being. You are an imperfect being. You are the imperfect human. You are imperfect in that you cannot see that you are imperfect. I am the one; I am the perfect *Hu*-man. I am not dead, you are dead. You are *dead* perfect.

I am perfect. I am the perfect being. I am the perfect human. I understand you. I understand your needs. I try to reach out. I try to speak to you. But you are incapable of hearing. You are paralysed by your thoughts. You are blinded by your goals. You have forgotten me. You have forgotten *hu-man*-ity.

Author's Note

To stand in silence when they should be protesting makes cowards out of men.
                                        Abraham Lincoln

Be the change you want to see in the world.
                                        Mahatma Gandhi

Humanity's Rage or How to Stop Blissful Ignorance and Start Worrying began as a product of adolescent angst, a teenager at odds with his world – an angry young man in an existential crisis. One observer saw it not as anger but rage, a rage that fluctuated between being inwardly, to the self, and outwardly, towards the world. It was about an individual needing to control his world so that his inner ideals would not collapse.

Initially entitled 'Encounters with X', the rage was supposed to be set in a psychiatric hospital. The piece presented itself as various encounters with an unnamed character – 'X'. Each encounter was to present an alternate view of reality, to question whether the 'alternate' was an alternate. The scene-setting would allow for the acceptable madness. However, it was never about madness and the scene-setting was a pretext to make a teenager's views acceptable to his peers.

Whilst the rage persisted, I was unable to express my feelings and thoughts to the world. That was until the means for this expression was realised. I had watched the film *Apocalypse Now*, in which Colonel Kurtz says:

> We train young men to drop fire on people. But their commanders won't allow them to write "*fuck*" on their aeroplanes, because it's obscene!

What was said was not absurd but the hypocrisy was. It was the character of Kurtz, and in particular this method of delivering his point, that inspired me to express myself in this piece (though the adolescent pieces – encounters I, II, IV, IX – were never in their current form).

The internal and external themes (the direction of the rage) were evident then. Internally (encounters XII, XIII, XV, XVI, XVIII): the loneliness and helplessness. Externally: the then concerns about the world – individualism, youth crime, feminism and the greed of capitalism in the mid-to-late 1980s. Perhaps the strongest themes are alienation with the status quo and the question as to why people had to suffer.

I remember, in my early teens, going to a library at school and opening a book about World War II.

On a double-page spread was a monochrome photograph of emaciated dead bodies – human beings with nothing but skin and bones dumped like rubbish and left to rot. I am not sure of which concentration camp it depicted, but I now assume it was Bergen-Belsen. But, nevertheless, it was more about what I had felt – a sense of shock. I was left asking myself questions: 'How could this have happened?' 'How could this be *allowed* to happen?' 'How could people *do* this?' One formidable question about humanity and suffering is still with me – 'Why?' Perhaps this proved to be the point of gestation of the rage.

Whilst I began to live with the rage, it was stimulated again in the latter part of the 1990s and 2000s, this time with a political tinge – a response to the suffocating and authoritarian policies of the government. The use of spin for political means, to hide truths and perpetuate mistruths, and the general pragmatism and complacency in accepting the latter, illustrated to me that much of society was indeed sleeping. Or at least they slept until their house prices and investments fell in value – self-interest seems to dictate over the concern for others.

During this time I also read *Soul Force* by M.K. Gandhi, edited by V. Geetha. This is a book about the writings of Mahatma Gandhi. The writings conveyed the essence of a great man, a truly remarkable person whose conviction is that you must act upon what you believe, and if you do not then you are therefore a coward. I felt I had to act upon my thoughts and feelings and continue with 'Encounters with X'.

Indeed, in expressing the inward and outward themes I tried to create a framework for this piece, in particular 'The Shade', where the themes run from the self to ever grander external issues (to others, to society, to economic systems, etc.):

    I Self: pain we inflict upon others without questioning
   II Self: our inaction when we see the pain of others
  III Others: infliction of pain by others without questioning
  IV Society: how misrepresentations are inflicted upon people*
   V Economic systems: economic systems inflicting pain on people**
  VI History and differences between peoples/cultures
 VII Governments
VIII Being perplexed at the above
  IX Culmination of I to VII

In 'The Shadow' I tried to express the impact on the self of the inability to control the environment/

---

* *The view of 'all men are rapists' mentioned in this encounter is a quote from 'The Women's Room' by Marilyn French. As it came from a leading thinker from the feminist social movement it thus had an impact on society.*

** *This is based on the society/economic system lived in; note, criticisms can apply to other systems.*

world. Whilst 'The Shade' had an external direction, 'The Shadow' has an internal one. They were intentionally placed in that order: cause and effect. It also benefits from concerns that progressively become insular:

    X Future: preventing ignorance
   XI External: overwhelming influence of the external on the individual
  XII Self: what is left when we give up on our humanity
 XIII Self: helplessness and loss of control
 XIV Self: questioning our humanity
  XV Self: loneliness without a common humanity
 XVI Self: numbing of existence
XVII Self: limits of tolerance
XVIII Self: reaching the limit

The Prelude, Postlude and encounter X were my response to those who were sleeping.

I should also like to acknowledge a reference I made to Octave Mirbeau's *Torture Garden*. In encounter II, I describe the torture of a man having his skin peeled off. I extended the original description of Mirbeau's crawling, as it had vivid imagery that would contrast with the self-questioning of inaction.

Please refer to the appendix for some additional notes, in <u>draft</u> form, that were not incorporated in encounter VII. Though I wanted to incorporate and refine them I did not think they related appropriately to the rest of the encounter.

M. K. Gandhi had outlined 'Science without Humanity' as one of his Seven Social Sins. I used this theme in an experimental piece, *Have They Forgotten Me?* It also followed the direction of concern over a certain aspect of humanity and is included here by way of thematic association.

Appendix: Unused Notes for Encounter VII

[DRAFT]

Whilst they clap at the film they view, clapping and celebrating the clinical efficiency of their weapon, they are in fact clapping and celebrating those children who have been blown to bits, clapping at the burning bodies of women and celebrating the dead still faces of men.

We close our eyes but we do not see the guts hanging out, we do not see the dismembered bodies.

Yes, when those clinical bombs kill our own children we will then shed tears. And once our tears have dried, we will look away yet again… we will do this because of the detachment we have to this clinical catharsis – a detachment so that we do not have to think about it, because we are selfish.

When those faces, when those victims – those children blown to bits – when they are laying there, someone – someone... will hold up some money and say it was for the benefit of mankind, for the benefit of humanity.

When we then see that money, we will close our eyes again and feel content in that justification, such that... such that when we shed those tears for our child, when we do this, as they lay dead in our arms, we will say to them the words of affection, the words of love – 'I love you'. We will say this, but we will not say, 'I looked the other way'. We will not say, 'I was content with that justification'. We will not say, 'I could not be bothered [to stand up and protest]' [about those clinical bombs]. We will definitely not say that, 'because of our inaction you have died'; 'because I valued that justification, because I valued that money, you have died; 'I loved that justification more than I loved you'.

Ingram Content Group UK Ltd.
Milton Keynes UK
UKHW020637190523
422019UK00014B/348